Where's Woody?

By Kristen L. Depken
Illustrated by Lori Tyminski and Jeremy Roberts

Random House New York

Copyright © 2012 Disney/Pixar. All rights reserved. Slinky® Dog is a registered trademark of Poof-Slinky, Inc.
© Poof-Slinky, Inc. Published in the United States by Random House Children's Books, a division of Random House, Inc.,
1745 Broadway, New York, NY 10019, and in Canada by Random House of Canada Limited, Toronto, in conjunction with
Disney Enterprises, Inc. Random House and the colophon are registered trademarks of Random House, Inc.
ISBN: 978-0-7364-2850-7
www.randomhouse.com/kids
MANUFACTURED IN MALAYSIA
10 9 8 7 6 5 4 3 2 1

Bonnie's toys are playing a game of hide-and-seek! It's Buzz's turn to seek.

"I've got the best hiding spot of all," declares Woody. "I bet you won't be able to find me, Buzz."

"All right, cowboy," says Buzz. "You're on!"

Buzz closes his eyes and begins to count to twenty. The toys hurry off to hide.

Buzz looks under Bonnie's toy basket first. Is that where Woody is hiding?

It's Rex!
"Thank goodness!" cries Rex. "It was dark under there."
"I'm sure we'll find Woody next," says Buzz.

Buzz sees Bonnie's cubbies.
"Over here!" he calls to Rex.
Is Woody hiding in a cubby?

It's Mr. Pricklepants!
"Well done, space ranger," says the stuffed hedgehog.
"Where *is* that cowboy?" asks Buzz.

The toys hear a noise coming from Bonnie's kitchen set.
"We've got him now!" says Buzz. "Come on!"
Rex and Mr. Pricklepants help Buzz climb up to Bonnie's
play microwave. Is Woody inside?

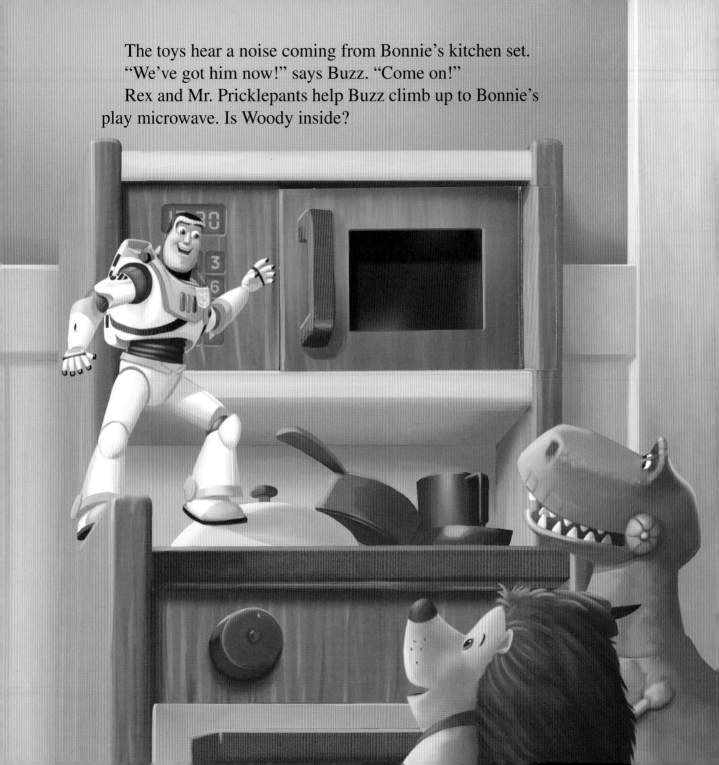

It's not Woody—it's Jessie and Bullseye!
"I can't believe I haven't found Woody yet!" says Buzz. "Where can he be?"
"We'll help you, Buzz!" says Jessie.

Buzz sees Bonnie's coat hanging on the chair. "Aha!" exclaims Buzz. He runs and looks in the pocket. Is Woody inside?

No—it's Dolly!
Buzz can't let Woody beat him at hide-and-seek! He tells everyone to split up.

Buzz checks Bonnie's bed. Who is behind the pillow?

Buzz can't believe that no one has found Woody!
Then the toys hear a muffled "Mmmppphh!"

"It's coming from that shoe box!" says Buzz.
Who's inside?

It's Woody—and he's stuck!
The toys help the cowboy out of Bonnie's shoe.
"Thanks, guys," says Woody. "I wish you had found me sooner!"
"It looks like you had the best hiding spot after all!" says Buzz.